THE OWL AND BILLY S

Martin Waddell has written many books for children, including the picture books *Farmer Duck* and *Can't You Sleep, Little Bear?*, both of which won the Smarties Book Prize. Among his many chapter books are *Little Obie and the Flood, Little Obie and the Kidnap, Fred the Angel, The Adventures of Pete and Mary Kate, The Dump Gang, My Aunty Sal and the Mega-sized Moose, Cup Final Kid* and *The Perils of Lord Reggie Parrot.*

The Owl and Billy Stories

Written by
MARTIN WADDELL

Illustrated by
PRISCILLA LAMONT

WALKER BOOKS
AND SUBSIDIARIES
LONDON • BOSTON • SYDNEY

A book for Catriona

First published 1998 by Walker Books Ltd
87 Vauxhall Walk, London SE11 5HJ

This edition published 1999

2 4 6 8 10 9 7 5 3 1

Text © 1998 Martin Waddell
Illustrations ©1998 Priscilla Lamont

The right of Martin Waddell to be identified as author
of this work has been asserted by him in accordance
with the Copyright, Designs and Patents Act 1988.

This book has been typeset in Plantin Light.

Printed in Great Britain by Clays Ltd, St Ives plc

British Library Cataloguing in Publication Data
A catalogue record for this book
is available from the British Library.

ISBN 0-7445-6036-5

CONTENTS

The Spaceman raised his hand and waved.

THE SECRET SPACEMAN

"I want to go to school *now*, Mum," Billy Ogle told his mum.

"Next week, Billy," said Mum. "School doesn't begin until next week."

"I don't want to wait until next week," said Billy.

"Well, you'll have to," said Mum.

Billy wasn't pleased.

"There's nobody to play with round here except Mrs Wilkins' baby Sam," he said. "Sam doesn't go to school."

Wilkins' baby was very small. Billy wheeled it sometimes with Mrs Wilkins, and he held the powder when she changed its nappy, but there wasn't much else he could do with it. It was a useless baby.

"I'm not going to play with Wilkins' baby," Billy told his mum. "I'm taking Owl for a ride instead."

Owl was Billy's best friend. Billy's mum had made Owl out of an old pillowcase and some stuffing. Owl was good fun to play with.

Owl and Billy went down Speck Street. They didn't walk. They went on Billy's tricycle. Owl sat on the handlebars, but he nearly fell off in surprise when they saw the van outside the Old People's flats.

It was a big green van, and some men were taking furniture out of it. They were moving the furniture into Mrs Bone's flat.

It was very old furniture, all wobbly-legged and patchy.

"I don't think Skinny Bone will be pleased," Billy told the furniture man.

"Who?" said the man.

"Mrs Bone," said Billy. "Mrs Bone has furniture already. I don't think she will be pleased if you put all that stuff on top of it."

Skinny Bone was a big fat lady. She chased people out of her garden. She was never pleased about anything.

"I dunno about that!" the man said, and he went on moving furniture. There was a clock with one hand missing, and a chair with broken springs, and an old cooker and…

"That's a motorbike!" gasped Billy.

Owl didn't know what a motorbike was, and Billy had to show him. It was a big black motorbike, with red demons painted on the side. It was too heavy to lift out of the van, and the furniture man had to put up a plank and wheel the motorbike down on to the road. Then the man put it in Skinny Bone's garden.

"Skinny Bone will start banging!" Billy told Owl.

Skinny Bone had a big stick and she banged it on the window when people went in her garden.

Owl told Billy he didn't like Skinny Bone when she banged.

"Mrs Bone's got a motorbike, Mum," Billy told his mum, when they got home. He made a lot of Skinny-Bone-on-her-motorbike-riding-round-the-garden noises up and down the kitchen to show Mum what Skinny Bone on a motorbike would be like.

"Mrs Bone's gone," said Mum.

"Gone?" said Billy.

"Not-Coming-Back-Gone-To-Australia-Gone," said Mum.

"Did she forget her bike?" asked Billy.

"The bike belongs to someone else," said Mum.

"What is it doing in Mrs Bone's garden if it belongs to someone else?" Billy asked.

"It isn't Mrs Bone's garden any more, Billy," said Mum. "Somebody new is coming to live in Mrs Bone's flat."

"Somebody who rides a motorbike," said Billy.

There were six Old People's flats, with six Old People in them. They were built with the ordinary Speck Street houses around them so that the Old People would have people to play with. Most of the Old People weren't much good at playing. They sat about in their gardens and were cross, and none of them rode motorbikes.

"Owl wants to see the motorbike again," Billy said, and Owl and Billy went off up Speck Street to see it.

"Stop," said Billy. "Look!"

Owl looked, and nearly fell off the

handlebars again.

"A Spaceman!" said Billy.

There was a Spaceman in Skinny Bone's flat. The Spaceman was dressed in black, and he had a big round space helmet on his head. He looked as if he had come down WHOOSH from Mars in a space rocket. Owl and Billy stood up on the wall of Skinny Bone's garden to get a better look.

The Spaceman saw them.

He looked at them through the window in his space helmet. Then he winked at Billy, and he raised his hand and waved. The hand was covered in a space glove, which was big and black and stretched halfway up his arm.

"Rubber arms!" gasped Billy, and Owl thought they were too.

"It might just be his space suit," said Billy after a minute. "And it might be rubber arms."

Owl thought they should ask the Spaceman, but Billy couldn't, because he wasn't allowed to speak to anyone Mum didn't know.

Owl and Billy went back home.

"There is a Spaceman in Mrs Bone's flat, with rubber arms," Billy told his mum. "Owl saw him."

"Is there?" said Mum, in her I-don't-believe-Billy voice.

"Owl says he's a Spaceman," said Billy. "Owl thinks the Spaceman has rubber arms, but I think they might be part of his space suit."

"What planet does he come from?" asked Mum, switching off the cleaner.

"Owl thinks Mars," said Billy.

"What do you think?" said Mum.

"Venus!" said Billy, who knew all about planets because he had a book about them.

"Not Watford?" said Mum. "That's what it said on the removal van. WATFORD in big red letters."

"Owl says the Spaceman comes from trillions of light years away," said Billy.

"Perhaps he stopped off at Watford on the way," said Mum. "Why don't you ask him?"

"I told Owl I wasn't allowed to speak to the Spaceman because I didn't know him," said Billy. "Do you know the Spaceman, Mum?"

"Yes, you can tell him Cousin Nora sent you," said Mum.

"Your name isn't Cousin Nora," Billy said.

"It isn't now," said Mum. "It used to be."

"Is Cousin Nora a sort of password, Mum?" Billy asked.

"That's right," said Mum. "You try it, and see what happens."

Owl and Billy rode back to the Old People's, on Billy's tricycle.

The Spaceman was standing in the garden, still wearing his space suit.

"Cousin Nora sent us," said Billy. And then he added, "It's a sort of password."

"I see," said the Spaceman.

"This is Owl," said Billy, showing Owl to the Spaceman. "Owl thinks that you are a Spaceman."

"How did he know?" asked the Spaceman.

"I told him that you had a space helmet," said Billy. "That's how he knew."

"Well spotted!" said the Spaceman.

"Are you a real Spaceman?" Billy asked. "A Spaceman from Watford?"

"That's right," said the Spaceman. "But don't tell! Nobody is supposed to know."

"Except me and Owl," said Billy.

"Correct," said the Spaceman.

"And my mum," said Billy.

"If you say so," said the Spaceman. "But absolutely nobody else!"

Then he got on to his motorbike and zoom-varoomed off down Speck Street, but before he went he hooted his horn three times.

"That must be a Space Signal!" Billy told Owl, and Owl said that proved the Spaceman was a spaceman.

"But we mustn't tell anyone," Billy said, and Owl said he wouldn't.

"Come and help me with the hoover," said Mum.

The Spaceman Pays a Visit

Next day, when Billy was having his breakfast, there was a loud noise.

VAROOM!

VAROOM! VAROOM!

"What's that?" asked Billy's dad, and he went to look out of the window.

VAROOM!

VAROOM! VAROOM!

"Some old codger fiddling with a motorbike," said Dad.

"Owl wants to know what a codger is, Dad," said Billy.

"Somebody who is very old," said Dad.

"Like you?" said Billy.

"No," said Dad. "Much older."

"Like the Old People," said Mum helpfully.

VAROOM!

VAROOM! VAROOM!

Billy didn't say anything, but he knew who the codger was. There was only one codger in Speck Street who went Varoom, and that was the Secret Spaceman.

"Wonder who he is?" Dad said. "I haven't seen that one around before."

"He's the one I told you about," said Mum. "My mum's cousin. He's moved down from Watford. Billy says he's a spaceman."

"Does he?" said Dad.

Billy didn't say anything. He was cross, and so was Owl. The Spaceman was a Special Secret, not to be told to anyone, and anyone included Dad.

Billy waited until Dad had gone off to

work, and then he was cross with Mum.

"You told on him!" he said.

"On who?" said Mum.

"The Spaceman," said Billy.

"Oh dear," said Mum.

"You weren't supposed to tell anyone that there was a Spaceman," said Billy.

"Only you and me and Owl and the Spaceman know, and you are only in it because we told you accidentally, before we knew it was a Special Secret."

"I don't suppose the Spaceman will mind your dad knowing," said Mum.

"He minds very much," said Billy. "It is Top Secret Space Information."

Owl said that it was too.

"Well, we won't tell your dad, then," said Mum.

"You've already told him," Billy said.

"I told him that there was a new tenant in

the Old People's and that I used to know him in Watford when I was little like you," Mum said. "I said that you said he was a spaceman, but your dad thinks you are only making it up."

"Owl says you'll have to promise not to tell again," Billy said.

"Tell Owl I promise," said Mum, and Owl said that was all right.

After breakfast Owl and Billy went for a ride on Billy's tricycle, and Owl wanted to visit the Spaceman, so they rang the Spaceman's doorbell.

"Who's that?" shouted a sleepy voice from inside the Spaceman's house.

"Owl and Billy," said Billy.

The Spaceman opened the door.

He hadn't got his helmet on, that was the first thing Billy noticed; and the second was that the Spaceman hadn't got much hair.

The top of his head was bald and shiny, like an apple, with little brown spots.

"You've got brown spots on your head," Billy told the Spaceman.

"Space rays!" said the Spaceman.

"Did they burn all your hair off?" asked Billy.

"It isn't all off," said the Spaceman.

"You haven't got very many hairs," said Billy, and the Spaceman didn't look very pleased.

"Owl thought you might come out to play," said Billy.

"Can't," said the Spaceman.

"Why not?" asked Billy.

"Receiving messages," said the Spaceman. "Messages from Outer Space."

"Oh," said Billy.

Owl wanted to know what kind of messages, so Billy asked the Spaceman.

"Messages like 'You've run out of milk'," said the Spaceman.

"Have you?" said Billy.

"Yes," said the Spaceman.

"I'll show you where to get some, if you like," said Billy.

Owl and Billy went to Mrs Jefferson's shop on the corner with the Spaceman to get some milk.

"Thank you very much," said the Spaceman, and he gave Billy 5p for not dropping the milk.

Owl and Billy went home.

"Where have you been?" Mum asked.

"We were visiting the Spaceman," Billy said, and he showed Mum the 5p.

"Oh dear," said Mum. "You mustn't pester him, Billy."

"I'm not," said Billy. "I was helping." And he told Mum about the Space Message, and not dropping the milk.

"That was very good of you, Billy," she said. "But you musn't go knocking on the Old People's doors and disturbing them."

"I only did it because Owl asked me to," Billy said.

"Yes, well," said Mum. "That's all right, but you must tell Owl he isn't to go disturbing Mr Bennet again."

"Who is Mr Bennet?" asked Billy. "Is he my Spaceman?"

"Yes," said Mum.

"Are you sure that's his name?" asked Billy, who thought that Mr Bennet was a funny name for a Spaceman.

"Yes," said Mum.

"I'm going to ask him if it really is," said Billy, hopping on his tricycle.

"Oh no you're not," said Mum. "You're going to help me with the dishes."

Billy helped with the dishes and Owl watched, and then Owl decided that he wanted to go and play with the Spaceman.

"Later, Billy," said Mum.

"Owl wants to go now," said Billy.

"Owl can't," said Mum. "Mr Bennet is an old man. I'm not sure that he wants to play with Owl all day."

"Shall I go and ask him, Mum?" Billy asked.

"No," said Mum.

Owl and Billy had to stay at home.

They stayed at home all morning and Billy played football with Owl. Owl wasn't much good at football and Billy won. Then they played races round the sitting room, and Billy won again. Then Sam came to play for half an hour while Mrs Wilkins went off to the shops, and Mum read Owl and Billy and Wilkins' baby a story.

"Can Owl go and see the Spaceman now, Mum?" Billy asked.

"No, Billy," said Mum.

Mrs Wilkins came back and had coffee with Mum, and she said, "Soon be going to school, Billy, now you are a big boy."

"Can't be too soon for Billy," Mum said. "He gets very bored playing by himself."

"I play with Owl," Billy said.

They had their dinner, and then Owl and Billy went for a tricycle ride, but the Spaceman wasn't there when they rode past his flat.

Owl wanted to ring the doorbell, in case the Spaceman was inside getting messages from Outer Space.

"Mum doesn't let us," Billy told him. Instead they had races up and down the pavement outside the Spaceman's flat. But the Spaceman didn't come out.

They went home, and Billy read Owl the story Mum had read to Sam. Billy knew nearly all the words.

Mum gave them biscuits, and Owl and Billy sat in the window and watched the Spaceman's garden, but the Spaceman didn't appear.

"Owl wants to go and see if the Spaceman's in his flat, Mum," Billy said.

"Not just now, Billy," said Mum. "Come and help me with the hoover."

"Owl doesn't want to," Billy said.

"You can do things that Owl doesn't want to," Mum said. "Owl doesn't give you orders."

"I don't want to either," said Billy.

"Thanks for nothing!" Mum said, and she went on hoovering.

Then…

Brrrrrrrrrrrr! Brrrrrrrrr! Brrrrrrrr! went

the doorbell, three times.

Mum went to open the door. It was the Spaceman.

"Hello, Mr Bennet!" Mum said, and she gave the Spaceman a big hug.

"Little Nora!" said the Spaceman.

"My mum isn't little!" said Billy, but nobody paid any attention to him. The Spaceman was giving Billy's mum her big hug back, and they started talking and talking and laughing.

"Hello," Billy said.

"Hello, you!" said the Spaceman, unhugging Mum.

"Have you come to play with us?" Billy asked.

"Now, Billy..." Mum began.

"Yes," said the Spaceman.

Billy and the Spaceman and Owl and Mum all sat down in the front room and played a guessing game, and then Billy showed the Spaceman his Woggly Man. The Spaceman made Woggly Man walk up and down on his knee and then Mum made some coffee. Afterwards Owl and Billy and Woggly Man and the Spaceman all went out into the back and Billy showed the Spaceman Owl's house, and how to stand on one leg.

The Spaceman said, "I've trouble enough standing up on two!" and Mum laughed.

"Time I went home," the Spaceman said.

"I want you to stay and play," said Billy.

"Poor Billy is waiting to start school," Mum said. "He has no one to play with."

"I haven't much time for playing," said the Spaceman. "But I tell you what. If Billy comes over to my house sometimes and gives three rings on the bell, he can help me with my work."

"Space Messages?" gasped Billy.

"And other things," said the Spaceman mysteriously. "Come back with me now, and I'll show you."

Owl and Billy went back with the Spaceman to his flat, and the Spaceman showed them some Secret Space Signals like this:

which means "YES"

and this

which means "NO"

and this

which means "I WANT TO THINK ABOUT IT".

They tried the signals out.

"Are you Billy?" the Spaceman asked, and Billy went

"Do you go to school yet?" the Spaceman asked, and Billy went

"Are you going to school soon?" the Spaceman asked, and Billy went

"Is Owl going too?" the Spaceman asked.

"I don't know," Billy said. "I don't know if owls can go to school."

"Then go " the Spaceman said.

"That means you want to think about it!"

And Billy did.

When he got home, he asked Mum if Owl could go to school.

"I don't think there are many Owls at school, Billy," Mum said. "But I expect the teacher won't mind if you take Owl for the first few days."

"Owl isn't sure if he wants to go to school,

Mum," Billy said. "He says we have the Spaceman to play with, and we don't need to go to school now."

"Owl's silly," said Mum. "You tell him how nice school is."

"I don't know how nice it is," said Billy.

"*Very* nice!" said Mum. "You'll really like it, Billy. Don't worry."

"I'm not," said Billy. "It was Owl who was worrying."

"Tomorrow you can go and play with the Spaceman again, Billy," said Mum. "Stop worrying about old school, and think about that."

Owl and Billy went upstairs to bed, and Owl asked Billy a lot of questions and Billy told him the answers using the Spaceman's Secret Signals. It was great fun, and Billy forgot all about going to school. So did Owl.

Billy counted ONE-TWO-THREE-
FOUR-FIVE again.

BILLY AND THE
SECRET MESSAGES

"Mum?" said Billy the next morning. "Mum, what is Watford?"

"It's a place, Billy. I used to live there, before I met your dad."

"Before?" said Billy.

"We weren't always Mum and Dad, Billy," said Mum. "I was a little girl and he was a little boy like you, and we grew up, and we met, and then we had a little boy of our own, called Billy."

"That's me," said Billy.

"Right," said Mum.

"And then you made Owl," said Billy.

"Exactly," said Mum.

VAROOM!

VAROOM! VAROOM!

"There goes Mr Bennet again!" said Mum. "Go and tell him he's making a lot of noise."

"All right," said Billy, and he got out his tricycle and took Owl down to the Old People's, where the Spaceman was varooming his motorbike.

"My mum says that you are making a lot of noise," Billy told the Spaceman.

"I know," said the Spaceman. He was lying on his back fiddling with some of the twiddly bits underneath his motorbike.

"Are you really called Mr Bennet?" Billy asked. "That's what people call me," said the Spaceman mysteriously.

Owl wanted to know what the Spaceman's real name was, so Billy asked him.

"Ah," said the Spaceman.

"Ah?" said Billy. "Ah is a funny name." Billy laughed at the funny name, and Owl did too.

"I didn't mean that Ah was my name," said the Spaceman. "I meant Ah-That-Would-Be-Telling."

Then he got up and sat on his motorbike, and tried the accelerator.

VAROOM! VAROOM!

"Fixed!" he said.

"Don't varoom it again, please," Billy said. "Owl's afraid that all the Old People will be complaining."

"I don't see anybody complaining," said the Spaceman.

"There's old Pinball," said Billy. "He is the one who sticks pins in footballs. Miss Henshawe is the one with the smelly cat and Miss Rice has no teeth and Henny Compton has no legs."

"No legs?" said the Spaceman.

"He has legs, sort of," said Billy. "They don't work properly. He's got a wheelchair. He's nice."

"I have come down to a funny planet!" said the Spaceman.

They went into the Spaceman's flat, and he flopped down in his armchair and closed his eyes.

"Are you going to sleep?" Billy asked.

"No," said the Spaceman. "I'm receiving messages."

"Oh," said Billy. "Can I do it?"

"No," said the Spaceman. "What you can do is try and keep very still until I open my eyes again, and then I'll tell you what the message is."

"Right," said Billy, and he kept very still, until he had counted up to five three times.

"I'm going to count to ten when I go to

school," he told the Spaceman.

"Do five again," said the Spaceman. "The message is just coming through."

Billy counted ONE-TWO-THREE-FOUR-FIVE again, and then Owl did it twice, and then Owl wouldn't do it any more.

"Owl is tired of counting," Billy said.

"That's all right," said the Spaceman. "I've got the message now."

"What message?" asked Billy.

"The message is: THERE IS ICE-CREAM IN THE FRIDGE," said the Spaceman.

"Is there?" said Billy.

"Well, there wasn't," said the Spaceman. "But if the message says there is now, I suppose there must be. Let's go and see."

There was.

It was raspberry. Billy liked it, and Owl liked it, although he gave most of his to Billy.

"How did the ice-cream get in the fridge?" Billy asked.

"Beamed down," said the Spaceman. "One minute it isn't there, and the next it just appears."

"Could you beam down some more?" asked Billy.

"Not today," said the Spaceman.

"Could I be a Spaceman?"

"No," said the Spaceman. "You belong down here. But you can be a Spaceman's Assistant, and help me."

"Good," said Billy.

"Wait," said the Spaceman. "I'm getting another message." He closed his eyes, and lay back in the chair.

"And…the…message…is…

IT IS TIME FOR OWL AND BILLY TO GO HOME NOW."

Billy thought about the Secret Message,

and he asked Owl about it. Owl wasn't pleased.

"Owl doesn't want to go home," Billy told the Spaceman.

"Then he won't find out why," said the Spaceman.

"Why what?"

"Why it is time for you to go home," said the Spaceman.

"I thought it was because you felt sleepy," said Billy.

"There's another reason," said the Spaceman. "You ask your mother about it. She'll know what it is."

Billy asked his mum when he got home.

"Quite right!" said Mum. "There is a reason!"

"Oh," said Billy. "What is it?"

"Because ... because your new schoolbag has just come," said Mum.

"OOOOOH!" said Billy.

It was a brilliant new schoolbag, blue and shiny, with bright red stripes down each side. It had thick green straps to fit over Billy's shoulders and there was even a special pocket at the front which Owl could sit in.

"I'm going to take it to show the Spaceman, Mum," Billy said.

"No, Billy," said Mum. "I'm sure the Spaceman needs a long, long nap after all those messages."

"They were TRUE too!" Billy said. "There *was* ice-cream in the fridge, and it *was* time I came home, because my schoolbag was here!"

"I think your Spaceman is very clever, Billy," said Mum.

"I think so too," said Billy.

And Owl thought that they were right.

Billy saw the Spaceman zoom-varooming off.

Owl Runs Away

"Today's a very important day!" Billy told the Spaceman on Thursday morning.

"Why?" said the Spaceman.

They were on their way back from Mrs Jefferson's shop on the corner where the Spaceman had been buying some Fizz Bombs because Spacemen like Fizz Bombs.

"I'm going to see my new school," said Billy.

"I see," said the Spaceman.

"Did you go to school?" Billy asked, because he wasn't certain if Spacemen went to school.

"Yes," said the Spaceman, and he gave Billy one of the Fizz Bombs.

"Where was your school?" said Billy.

"Mars," said the Spaceman.

"Mine's on the Newton Road."

"Owl says he doesn't like my new school," Billy said.

"But *you* will," said the Spaceman.

"How do you know I will?" asked Billy.

"Got a message about it," said the Spaceman. "It said:

BILLY WILL LIKE SCHOOL."

"Oh," said Billy.

He told his mum about it on the way to see his new school that afternoon.

"I'm not surprised," said Mum. "It's a very nice school."

"I know it is," said Billy. "But Owl doesn't like it."

"Owl hasn't seen it yet," said Mum, as they turned in the gate.

Billy took Owl out of his schoolbag, so that

he could see what the new school was like.

Billy's new school wasn't new, it was old. It was made of red bricks, and it had two chimneys, and a door with a hall where Billy could hang his coat. Miss Murphy showed him where his coat would go, and she wrote out a label:

BILLY OGLE

Billy stuck the label above the coat-peg which was just beside the door of the classroom.

There was a sandpit and easels and cushions and desks and a water-play tray and a slide and a little tiny garden with things growing in it.

"This is where you'll sit, Billy," said Miss Murphy.

Owl and Billy sat down.

"Who is this you've brought with you?" Miss Murphy asked.

"Owl," said Billy. "I'm going to marry Owl when I grow up."

"What does Owl think about that?" Miss Murphy asked.

"Owl's going to marry me too," said Billy. "Then we'll belong to each other."

"I hope I'm invited to the wedding," said Miss Murphy.

"We're inviting our friends," said Billy, who wasn't very certain what a wedding was, but thought it was probably something like a birthday.

"It's my birthday soon," Billy told Miss Murphy.

"Sunday," said Mum.

"I'm having a party," said Billy, but he didn't say anything about inviting Miss Murphy to it, because he wasn't certain if she was one of his friends.

Then they saw the playground, and the

dining room where Billy would have his lunch, and they looked at the pictures on the walls, and then Miss Murphy said, "Bye-bye, Billy, see you on Monday morning."

Billy and Mum walked home.

"Your new school is nice, Billy," Mum said. "Lots of things to play with."

"Y-e-s," said Billy.

"And there'll be lots of children too. Boys and girls."

"Where were they?" Billy asked.

"They'd all gone home," Mum said. "We came down after school, so that you could see it."

"Did they all go home because they didn't like it?" Billy asked.

"They all went home because it was time to go home," said Mum. "Everybody goes home after school."

Billy thought about it. It was a long, long

way to school from his house, and a long, long way back.

"I'm not sure I could find it," he said uneasily.

"I'll take you there," said Mum.

"And bring me back?" asked Billy.

"Every day," said Mum.

"Every single day?" said Billy, who didn't at all like the idea of going to school every single day.

"Except Saturdays and Sundays," said Mum. "And there are holidays as well. Weeks and weeks of days when you don't go to school at all."

When they got home, Billy went to tell the Spaceman about it.

"Well?" said the Spaceman. "Was my message right?"

"Y-e-s," said Billy.

"My Space Messages are always right,"

the Spaceman said.

"Owl didn't like it one bit," said Billy.

"What didn't he like?" said the Spaceman.

"School," said Billy.

"I'll have to speak to Owl about that," said the Spaceman. "Where is he, anyway?"

"In my schoolbag," said Billy, and he opened his schoolbag to take Owl out of it but...

OWL WASN'T THERE!

"What's the matter?" said the Spaceman.

"Owl's gone!" said Billy, holding his schoolbag open.

"I expect you left him at home," said the Spaceman.

"I didn't," said Billy.

"Perhaps your mum has him?" said the Spaceman.

"No she hasn't," said Billy.

They went to Billy's house.

"Owl?" said Mum. "Didn't you bring him home, Billy?"

Billy shook his head.

"Perhaps he dropped out on the way?" said the Spaceman.

"He's run away!" said Billy, feeling tears well up in his eyes.

"No he hasn't," said Mum.

"Of course he hasn't," said the Spaceman. "Hang on a bit, and I'll go and look for him!"

The Spaceman went back to the Old People's and put on his Spacesuit and the next thing Billy saw was him zoom-varooming off down the road on his motorbike.

"Here's Woggly Man come to see you," Billy's mum said, and she gave Billy Woggly Man, but Billy didn't want Woggly Man, and he threw Woggly Man over the sofa.

"I'm sure Owl will turn up, Billy," Mum said.

"He's run away," Billy said.

"No he hasn't."

"He's run away because he didn't like school," said Billy. "He didn't like Miss Murphy and he doesn't want to go there every day."

Mum made Billy an orange drink, and gave him some biscuits, but Billy didn't eat any. He didn't feel like biscuits. He wanted Owl.

Then…

Zoom Varoom!

The Spaceman's motorbike came whizzing down the road, and pulled up in front of Billy's house.

Billy ran to the door to let him in.

"Have you got Owl?" he asked.

"No," said the Spaceman. "No. I haven't

got him, BUT..."

"But what?" asked Billy.

"BUT I got a message," said the Spaceman.

"A Space Message?" asked Billy hopefully. "A Space Message about Owl?"

"Right," said the Spaceman. "I got a Space Message saying:

'OWL IS ALL RIGHT AND HE'LL BE HERE IN A MINUTE'."

"I hope you're right," said Billy's mum. "Are you certain this Space Message is going to work, Mr Bennet?"

"Spaceman's Honour," said the Spaceman, and he crossed his thumbs, like this

"Is that one of your secret signs?" Billy asked. The Spaceman didn't say anything, but he went which is the Secret Sign for "Yes".

"What's this all about?" asked Mum.

"It's Top Secret Space Information, Mum," said Billy. "You're not allowed to know."

Then…

BRRRRRNNNNGGGG BRRRRRRNNNNGGGGG!

went the doorbell.

"Better go and see who that is, Billy," said the Spaceman.

Billy opened the door, and it was his new teacher, Miss Murphy and OWL!

"Owl came back to school to see me, Billy," Miss Murphy said. "He wanted to be absolutely certain that you'd be all right, and I told him you would be. Now I've brought him back."

Billy took Owl from her.

"Say thank you to Miss Murphy, Billy," said Mum.

"Thank you, Miss Murphy," said Billy, uncertainly.

Then Mum thanked Miss Murphy and the Spaceman thanked Miss Murphy and they went out to the door to see Miss Murphy off in her car.

Billy stayed on the sofa with Owl.

Mum came back into the house, and closed the door behind her.

"Don't you go leaving Owl behind you again, Billy!" she said. "You're getting to be a big boy. You've got to learn to look after things."

Billy cuddled Owl.

"Cheer up," Mum said.

"Owl can't talk, Mum," Billy said.

"You're always telling me he can," said Mum.

"Only to me," said Billy.

"So?" said Mum.

"Not Miss Murphy."

"Miss Murphy was very kind coming all this distance out of her way to bring Owl back to you, Billy," said Mum.

"Owl doesn't like her," said Billy. "Owl doesn't talk to her."

"Tell Owl...." Mum began, and then she said, "Oh, I don't know what you tell Owl. I get fed up with Owl sometimes."

And she went out of the room.

That night, when Billy was getting tucked up in bed, he said, "Mum!"

"Yes, Billy?"

"Owl isn't real, Mum. Owl's made of a pillowcase, isn't he?"

"Yes, Billy," said Mum.

"So he couldn't talk to Miss Murphy, could he? He only talks to me, because I'm the one you made him for."

"I suppose that's right," said Mum.

Billy thought about it.

"Miss Murphy tells lies, Mum," he said. "Miss Murphy said Owl talked to her, and he didn't, because he's made of a pillowcase and he only talks to me."

"Maybe Owl did tell her something, Billy," Mum said.

"How?" Billy demanded.

"I don't know," said Mum. "Maybe some magic way. I think Owl told her you thought you might not like school either, and you were worried about it. And I think she brought Owl back here specially so he could tell you not to worry, because Miss Murphy is your friend."

"Is she?" asked Billy.

"I think so," said Mum. "Why don't we ask Owl?"

And they did.

And Owl whispered something back to

Billy, but Mum didn't know what it was, because only Billy could hear it.

"Well?" Mum said.

"Owl says Miss Murphy is my friend, Mum," said Billy.

"I thought he would," said Mum.

It was a great birthday party.

BILLY'S BIRTHDAY

Billy woke up very early on Sunday morning, because it was his birthday. Nobody else was awake, not even Owl. Billy had to wake Owl up to tell him, and Owl was very pleased, because he had been waiting for Billy's birthday for a long time.

Owl and Billy went down to tell Billy's mum and dad.

"Huh? Wassat?" Billy's dad said, peering out from under the bedclothes.

"My birthday!" said Billy.

"Oooo-aaah!" groaned Dad, and he yawned sleepily.

"Happy Birthday to me!" said Billy, and Dad picked him from beside the bed and snuggled him in beside Mum.

"Happy Birthday, Billy," Mum whispered sleepily. "Now go back to sleep."

Billy couldn't get back to sleep, but he tried. He tried very hard, but Owl didn't try. Owl was too excited.

Owl wanted to play.

Owl played pulling the bedclothes, and then he played walking up Billy, and then he played walking up Mum, and then he played tickling Dad.

"Okay!" said Dad. "I surrender!" and he got out of bed.

"What time is it?" muttered Mum.

"Six o' clock," said Dad. "Come on. We may as well pretend to be awake even if we aren't. You get the tea, and I'll get Billy's presents."

"You get the tea," said Mum. "I'll get Billy's presents!"

Billy got lots of presents.

There was a Big Space Lego set from Mum and a trumpet from Dad and a new coat from Aunt Paula and a Twisty Game from Uncle James and a boiled egg with a face on from Woggly Man and a new jumper from the Wilkins and a book from Sam and a toffee apple from Owl.

"Whose idea was that?" Mum said.

"Owl's, of course," said Dad. "With a little help from me."

"Don't eat it in bed, Billy!" warned Mum. "You'll get the bedclothes sticky."

Billy went downstairs and ate Owl's toffee apple on the sofa, while he was playing the Twisty Game.

Then the postman came.

There was a Happy Birthday card from Mum and Dad and Owl and Woggly Man and another from the Wilkins. There was one from Miss Murphy at the school, and there was a card from Henny Compton, with 50p taped inside.

"You'll have to go across and thank Henny for it, Billy," Mum said.

And then she sat down on the sofa, where she stuck.

"What am I sticking to?" she demanded.

"Owl thinks it might be toffee apple," Billy said.

"Get your father!" Mum said. "He brought it into the house, he can clean it off the sofa."

"It wasn't Dad who got me the toffee apple, Mum," said Billy. "It was Owl."

"Can Owl clean sofas?" Mum asked.

"No," said Billy.

"Then get your father!" said Mum.

Dad started cleaning the sofa, and Mum went upstairs to clean her dress and Owl and

Billy went across the road to say thank you to Henny Compton for the 50p.

"Hello," Henny said, drawing his wheelchair back from the door to let Billy in.

"Hello," said Billy. "Mum said I was to say Thank-You-For-The-50p-And-The-Lovely-Card and you can come to my party this afternoon, if you want to. It's at three o'clock and there's jelly."

"I like jelly," said Henny.

"If you're coming, bring your wheelchair," said Billy.

"I'll have to," said Henny.

"Good," said Billy. "I have a friend who doesn't know about wheelchairs. I want him to see it."

"Who?" said Henny.

"The Spa..." began Billy, and then he stopped and said, "Mr Bennet," because the Spaceman was Top Secret Space

Information, that Henny wasn't allowed to know about.

"Owl wants to see it too," Billy added.

"Owl's seen it before," Henny said. Henny knew Owl well. Owl had been for rides in his wheelchair.

"He wants to see it *again*," said Billy.

Then Billy went home.

It was a great Birthday Party.

Sam was sick all over the carpet and Dad burnt himself lighting the birthday candles and Mrs Wilkins got toffee apple on her skirt. (It couldn't have come from the sofa because Dad had cleaned it.) Henny's wheelchair went over Auntie Paula's foot and Auntie Paula was very rude and Billy and Owl and Woggly Man laughed and Mum said they shouldn't.

The best bit was the Spaceman.

The Spaceman brought Billy a Special Spacesuit made of shiny stuff. It had a belt and badge and a space helmet and a ray gun.

"Do you like it, Billy?" the Spaceman asked, and Billy went

Billy ray gunned Sam and Mrs Wilkins and Mum and Dad and Woggly Man and Owl and Henny Compton's wheelchair and the jelly and the orangeade and the sandwiches and the little cakes with hats on.

"Don't ray gun me, Billy," warned the Spaceman, and Billy went

Then they had their tea, and Sam and Mrs Wilkins and Henny Compton went home, and then it was time to go to bed.

"I want the Spaceman to put me to bed, Mum," Billy said, and the Spaceman did. Billy got up on the Spaceman's shoulders and they zoomed up the stairs like a space rocket, and then they had to zoom down again to get Owl.

"What about Woggly Man?" said Mum.

"Woggly Man doesn't sleep in my bed any more," said Billy, but the Spaceman carried Woggly Man upstairs as well.

"Poor Woggly Man," said the Spaceman, putting Woggly Man into the playbox. "I hope you aren't lonely in there."

"Owl says he isn't," said Billy.

"How does Owl know?" said the Spaceman. "Owl isn't lonely. Owl is in a nice comfy bed with you, not all alone in a playbox."

"Owl knows," said Billy.

"Owl doesn't know everything, Billy," said the Spaceman, sitting down on the end of the bed. "Lots of people get lonely."

"Like old Henny?" said Billy.

"Not just old people, Billy," said the Spaceman. "Think about it!"

And Billy made the secret sign

The Spaceman went away, and Mum came up to tuck Billy in.

"Mum," said Billy. "Is the Spaceman lonely sometimes?"

"I expect he is, Billy," said Mum.

"Like Woggly Man," said Billy. "Woggly Man is lonely, because Owl said there wasn't room for him in my bed."

"Owl's wrong!" said Mum. "There's plenty of room. Get Owl to move over!"

Billy moved Owl over, and Woggly Man got in.

"Now he won't be lonely, will he?" said Mum.

"Not a bit!" said Billy.

Billy couldn't get to sleep.

BILLY AND THE MONSTER

It was Sunday afternoon, the Sunday before Going-to-School-Monday.

"Nice new clothes for going to school, Billy!" Mum said.

The new clothes were all laid out on the bed. There were two pairs of trousers, and two shirts, and two jumpers.

"You'll look great," said Mum.

Billy looked at them.

"Owl says I'll be roasted if I have to wear two of everything," he said.

"Then Owl is very silly!" said Mum. "You only wear one pair of trousers, and one jumper, and one shirt at a time, the rest are spares."

And she put Billy's new clothes on him.

Billy went downstairs and showed Dad, and then Owl said that they should go and show the Spaceman, and Mum said they could.

Owl and Billy went to the Spaceman's house and rang three times on the bell, because that was another kind of Secret Signal to let the Spaceman know who was at the door before he came to answer it.

"These are my new clothes for going to school in," Billy told the Spaceman. "Owl doesn't like them."

"I think Owl is jealous," said the Spaceman.

"Owl likes my spacesuit better," said Billy. "The one you gave me for my birthday. It has a ray gun. If I'd had my ray gun with me I could have shot the Monster in the hall."

"What monster?" said the Spaceman.

"Owl says there was a Space Monster in the hall, outside your door," said Billy. "I could have shot him with my ray gun!"

"What was he like?" asked the Spaceman.

"Big," said Billy. "And hairy and nasty!"

"Where did he go?" asked the Spaceman. "He isn't still there, is he?"

"I don't know," said Billy.

They looked out in the hall, but the big hairy Space Monster wasn't there.

"Spacesuits are for fighting Space Monsters in," Billy said. "I would have fought him if I'd had my spacesuit on. Spacesuits are for adventures."

"Like your new clothes," said the Spaceman.

"My new clothes are for going to school," Billy said.

"Going to school is an adventure," said the Spaceman.

"I bet there aren't any Space Monsters there!" said Billy.

"You never know with Space Monsters," said the Spaceman.

Billy went home.

"Early bed, Billy," said Mum, after tea. "Big day tomorrow."

"New school," said Dad.

Billy didn't say anything.

He went upstairs with Mum and had a Special Bath with Mum's smelly soap, and Owl fell in.

Owl got wet, but he didn't drown because Billy saved him. Billy was afraid that Owl would catch cold but Mum said he wouldn't. She dried Owl with the hairdryer while Dad was reading Billy his story.

Billy and Owl and Woggly Man got into bed, though Owl had to stay on a towel down at the far end because he was still a bit damp.

Mum gave Owl a Special Kiss to make up for it, and Billy and Woggly Man got one too.

"Keep the light on, Mum," Billy said, and Mum said she would.

Billy couldn't get to sleep. He had to go downstairs to get a drink for Woggly Man and then he had to go down again to get something to keep Owl warm and then he left his ray gun behind, and he had to go down for it.

"What do you want your ray gun for, Billy?" Dad asked.

"The Monster," said Billy.

"What Monster?"

"There's a big hairy nasty Space Monster!" Billy said.

"No there isn't," said Dad.

"Yes there is," said Billy. "The Spa... Mr Bennet knows all about it!"

Dad told Mum.

"You're not afraid of a silly Space Monster, Billy!" Mum said.

"Owl's afraid of it," said Billy. "And it isn't silly. I saw it at the Spaceman's."

"I'll have to talk to the Spaceman about this," said Mum, and she went straight over to his flat and came back with him.

"Hello, Billy," said the Spaceman. "What's all this about a Monster?"

Billy didn't say anything. He just held on to Owl, because Owl was frightened of the Space Monster.

"I think maybe Owl imagined the Space Monster, Billy," said Mum.

"No he didn't," said Billy.

"What was this Monster like, Billy?" the Spaceman said.

"Big and hairy and nasty," said Billy.

"How nasty?" said the Spaceman.

"Black teeth and red eyes!" said Billy.

"Oh," said the Spaceman. "That's all right then."

"Why?" said Billy.

"It's a Go-Away Monster," said the Spaceman.

"Go-Away?" said Billy.

"Yes," said the Spaceman. "You just look at it and then you make a Secret Signal like this and it goes away!"

"Are you sure?" said Billy.

"Certain sure!" said the Spaceman. "Those Go-Away Monsters are real scaredy cats!"

"I'm not," said Billy. "I'm brave."

"Owl was the one who was frightened," said Mum. "Isn't that right, Billy?"

"Yes," said Billy.

"You tell Owl not to be frightened any more, Billy," said the Spaceman, and he went home.

"Mum," said Billy, when Mum was putting him to bed. "Mum, is Mr Bennet a Spaceman really?"

"I'm sure I don't know, Billy," said Mum. "What do you think?"

"Owl thinks he might be making it up," said Billy. "But I think he's a Spaceman."

"I like him either way," said Mum.

"So do I," said Billy.

Miss Murphy helped them to dress up.

Billy Goes to School

Monday was Going-to-School-Day.

Mum and Billy and Owl went off to school, leaving Woggly Man at home, all alone.

"Woggly Man wants to come too, Mum," Billy said. "Owl told me so. Can I bring him?"

"No," said Mum. "Only Owl."

"Why?"

"There wouldn't be room in school if the children brought all their friends with them," said Mum.

Billy and Owl waved to Woggly Man who was sitting in the front room window where he could see them.

"Can I show the Spaceman my new school shoes?" Billy asked, when they were passing the Spaceman's flat, but Mum said the Spaceman wouldn't be up yet.

They went to school.

There were lots of children at school, and most of them were bigger than Billy, but he didn't mind because Mum came in with him, and helped him to hang up his coat on the peg where his name was.

Then Miss Murphy came.

She was very nice. She took Owl and Billy to Billy's special seat and they made another special seat for Owl, on a cushion.

There were other new children, just like Billy. Some of them were fat and some of them were thin and one of them had red trousers. His name was Sam, like Wilkins' baby. He sat next to Billy, but Owl didn't like him.

Miss Murphy brought a girl over to Billy and Sam.

"This is Annie," said Miss Murphy. "Annie is going to show you all the things we do."

Annie did.

There were lots of things to do.

Billy and Annie and Sam played with the water-tray, and then they worked with the sand, and then they had their rest, and then Miss Murphy read a story, and then there were bricks, and then it was break.

"Will Mum come now?" Billy asked Miss Murphy.

"Not now," said Miss Murphy. "Later." And then she helped Billy and Sam and Annie to dress up, and they went in the little house with the blue door, and Billy and Sam made tea while Annie was out working.

Annie got Billy some cars from the car

box, and they put them on Miss Murphy's road, which ran over two whole tables, and they went round and round the roads. Then they had another story, and a song, and then they had dinner in the Little Ones' Dining Room. After that they went out to play and then they went in again and Miss Murphy talked a lot, and then it was time to go home.

"Where's Mum?" said Billy.

Mum came through the door. She was the first in of all the Mums and Dads and she met Annie and Sam.

"Sam's my best friend," said Billy, when they got outside.

"Good," said Mum.

"Annie's my next best!" said Billy.

"She looks nice," said Mum.

"Mary Rowen fell in the mud," said Billy, but Mum wasn't paying any attention. She was looking for something.

"I think you've forgotten something, Billy," she said.

"No I haven't," said Billy, because he knew he had his anorak hanging up on its peg and his schoolbag on his back, with his pencils in it.

"Yes you have," said Mum. "You've forgotten Owl!"

They had to go all the way back into School to get Owl, who'd moved up on to Miss Murphy's desk where he was waiting for Billy.

They went home and Billy had a warm drink and then the Spaceman came.

"Hello, Billy," he said. "How's school?"

"Great," said Billy, because it was, and he told the Spaceman all about Sam and Annie and Mary Rowen falling in the mud and what the Little Ones' Dining Room was like and what he had for dinner.

"What did Owl think?" the Spaceman said.

Billy thought a bit. "Owl didn't like it very much," he said.

"Oh dear," said Mum. "Why not?"

"Owl had no one to play with," said Billy.

"I thought he played with you?" said the Spaceman.

"I was busy," Billy said. "You have to be busy at school learning useful things."

"I see," said the Spaceman. And then he closed his eyes and had a Space Message. It said: THERE'S A SURPRISE UNDER THE CUSHION.

And there was! It was a bag of sweets.

"Not sweets!" said Mum. "You'll rot Billy's teeth."

"These sweets are for Owl," said the Spaceman.

"You'll rot Owl's teeth then," said Mum.

"Owl hasn't got any teeth," said Billy.

"But I'm sure he'd like some sweets to cheer him up," said the Spaceman. "He's been missing Billy all day, like me."

"I'll come and see you every day!" Billy said.

"Thank you very much," said the Spaceman, and he went home.

Dad came home and Billy told him all about school and then they had their tea and then Dad read him a story and then Owl and Billy went up to bed, and Mum brought Woggly Man up afterwards.

"Here's poor old Woggly Man, Billy," she said. "He's been very lonely all day, and he thinks you've forgotten him."

She put Woggly Man in bed, beside Billy and Owl.

"Owl was lonely too," said Billy, "because I was too busy to play with him."

"I expect he was," said Mum. "There isn't

really much for Owl to do at school, is there? I think he should stay at home tomorrow, and keep Woggly Man company. Then they could play with each other."

Billy asked Owl, and Owl said it was a very good idea, and Woggly Man thought it was a good idea too.

Mum went downstairs, but she forgot to bring up a drink of water for Owl, so Billy had to go down and get it. Then he had to go down again, to get another for Woggly Man.

"We're not having this every night, Billy," said Mum, and she carried him upstairs again, and tucked him in.

"Mum," said Billy.

"Yes?" said Mum.

"Maybe I shouldn't go to school either," said Billy. "Maybe I should stay at home with Owl and Woggly Man. That's what Owl thinks."

"But you liked it!" Mum said. "You know you did. You liked Annie, and Sam, and Miss Murphy, and all the things to play with, didn't you?"

"Owl wants me to stay at home," said Billy. "He wants somebody real to play with, not just Woggly Man."

Mum thought about it.

"I think I know who Owl would like to play with, Billy," Mum said.

"Who?" said Billy. And Mum told him.

Next morning, when Billy was getting ready for School, he put Owl and Woggly Man in a carrier bag, and when Billy and Mum were going past the Spaceman's house they put the carrier bag in the porch, where the Spaceman would be bound to see it.

"I hope they'll be all right, Mum," Billy said.

"Of course they will," said Mum. "Owl and Woggly Man and the Spaceman will all play together, and then none of them will be lonely."

"But they'll all miss me, won't they?" said Billy.

"Of course they will," said Mum. "But you'll see them when you get home!"

Owl and Woggly Man and the Spaceman were all in the Spaceman's garden when Billy got home, and Billy jumped over the Spaceman's wall and joined them.

"We're having a Billy-Getting-Home-From-School-Picnic!" the Spaceman said.

"Can we have one every day?" Billy asked.

"So long as it isn't wet, Billy," Mum said, looking over the fence.

"Wait a minute," said the Spaceman. "Wait. I'm getting a Message. And the Message says:

IF IT IS WET YOU CAN HAVE YOUR PICNIC INSIDE."

Owl thought that was a great idea.

They had crisps, sweets, apples and fizzy lemonade. Billy finished Owl's for him.

"Mum," said Billy, when Mum was putting him to bed. "I like school, Mum."

"Good," said Mum.

"And Owl and Woggly Man like playing with the Spaceman," said Billy.

"I'm sure he likes having them," said Mum.

"So he won't be lonely," said Billy.

"That's right," said Mum.

"Good," said Billy, and he curled up warm and snug under the blankets, with Owl under one arm and Woggly Man under the other, and they all went to sleep.

THE KIT STORIES
Jane Gardam

Kit lives on a farm with her farmer father, her mother and her little sister Lisa. Her parents often call her *the* Kit, because they think she's a bit of a baby, crying at silly things like beetles or putting her foot in a cow-pat. But Kit can be very brave and sensible too, as she shows when Geoffrey, the fierce bull, gets loose. The most exciting moment in Kit's life, though, is when she's invited to London to be a bridesmaid. Read about her adventures in these lively stories by an award-winning author.

THE ADVENTURES OF PETE AND MARY KATE
Martin Waddell

One week Pete has to go to his gran's flat every day. He likes his gran and her stories, but there's no one to play with and Pete soon gets bored. Gran says he can play with her old doll, Mary Kate, but Pete doesn't think that will be much fun. He's wrong though! For Mary Kate is a special doll, who loves adventures, and soon she and Pete are climbing Armchair Mountain, bearbooing Big Bears, sailing across Carpet Sea and having a very exciting time indeed!

MORE WALKER STORY BOOKS
For You to Enjoy

☐ 0-7445-5416-0   *The Adventures of Pete and
Mary Kate*
by Martin Waddell/Terry Milne   £3.50

☐ 0-7445-5456-X   *The Kit Stories*
by Jane Gardam/Paul Howard   £3.50

☐ 0-7445-4381-9   *One for Me, One for You*
by Rita Phillips Mitchell/
Paul Howard   £3.50

☐ 0-7445-3684-7   *Willa and Old Miss Annie*
by Berlie Doherty/Kim Lewis   £3.50

☐ 0-7445-6024-1   *Fiona Says...*
by Diana Hendry/Dave McTaggart £3.50

☐ 0-7445-5482-9   *In Crack Willow Wood*
by Sam McBratney/Ivan Bates   £3.50

☐ 0-7445-3186-1   *The Stone Mouse*
by Jenny Nimmo/Helen Craig   £3.50

☐ 0-7445-3089-X   *Here Comes Tod!*
by Philippa Pearce/Adriano Gon   £3.50